I'm Going To READ!

These levels are meant only as guides;
you and your child can best choose a book that's right.

Level 1: Kindergarten–Grade 1 . . . Ages 4–6
- word bank to highlight new words
- consistent placement of text to promote readability
- easy words and phrases
- simple sentences build to make simple stories
- art and design help new readers decode text

Level 2: Grade 1 . . . Ages 6–7
- word bank to highlight new words
- rhyming texts introduced
- more difficult words, but vocabulary is still limited
- longer sentences and longer stories
- designed for easy readability

Level 3: Grade 2 . . . Ages 7–8
- richer vocabulary of up to 200 different words
- varied sentence structure
- high-interest stories with longer plots
- designed to promote independent reading

Level 4: Grades 3 and up . . . Ages 8 and up
- richer vocabulary of more than 300 different words
- short chapters, multiple stories, or poems
- more complex plots for the newly independent reader
- emphasis on reading for meaning

LEVEL 3

2 4 6 8 10 9 7 5 3 1

Published by Sterling Publishing Co., Inc.
387 Park Avenue South, New York, NY 10016
Text © 2006 by Harriet Ziefert Inc.
Illustrations © 2006 by Rich Rossi
Distributed in Canada by Sterling Publishing
c/o Canadian Manda Group, 165 Dufferin Street,
Toronto, Ontario, Canada M6K 3H6
Distributed in the United Kingdom by GMC Distribution Services,
Castle Place, 166 High Street, Lewes, East Sussex, England BN7 1XU
Distributed in Australia by Capricorn Link (Australia) Pty. Ltd.
P.O. Box 704, Windsor, NSW 2756, Australia

I'm Going To Read is a trademark of Sterling Publishing Co., Inc.

Library of Congress Cataloging-in-Publication Data

Ziefert, Harriet.
  Ouch! / Harriet Ziefert ; pictures by Rich Rossi.
    p. cm.—(I'm going to read)
  Summary: Jon falls off of his bicycle but is less than enthusiastic
about receiving treatment for the cut on his forehead.
  ISBN-13: 978-1-4027-3424-3
  ISBN-10: 1-4027-3424-7
  [1. Wounds and injuries—Fiction. 2. Sutures—Fiction. 3. Medical care—
  Fiction.] I. Rossi, Richard, 1960– ill. II. Title. III. Series.

PZ7.Z487Ou 2006
[E]—dc22   2005034361

Sterling ISBN-13: 978-1-4027-3424-3
ISBN-10: 1-4027-3424-7

For information about custom editions, special sales, premium and
corporate purchases, please contact Sterling Special Sales
Department at 800-805-5489 or specialsales@sterlingpub.com.

I'm Going To READ!™

OUCH!

Pictures by Rich Rossi.

Sterling Publishing Co., Inc.
New York

"I fell! I fell!"
cried Jon.

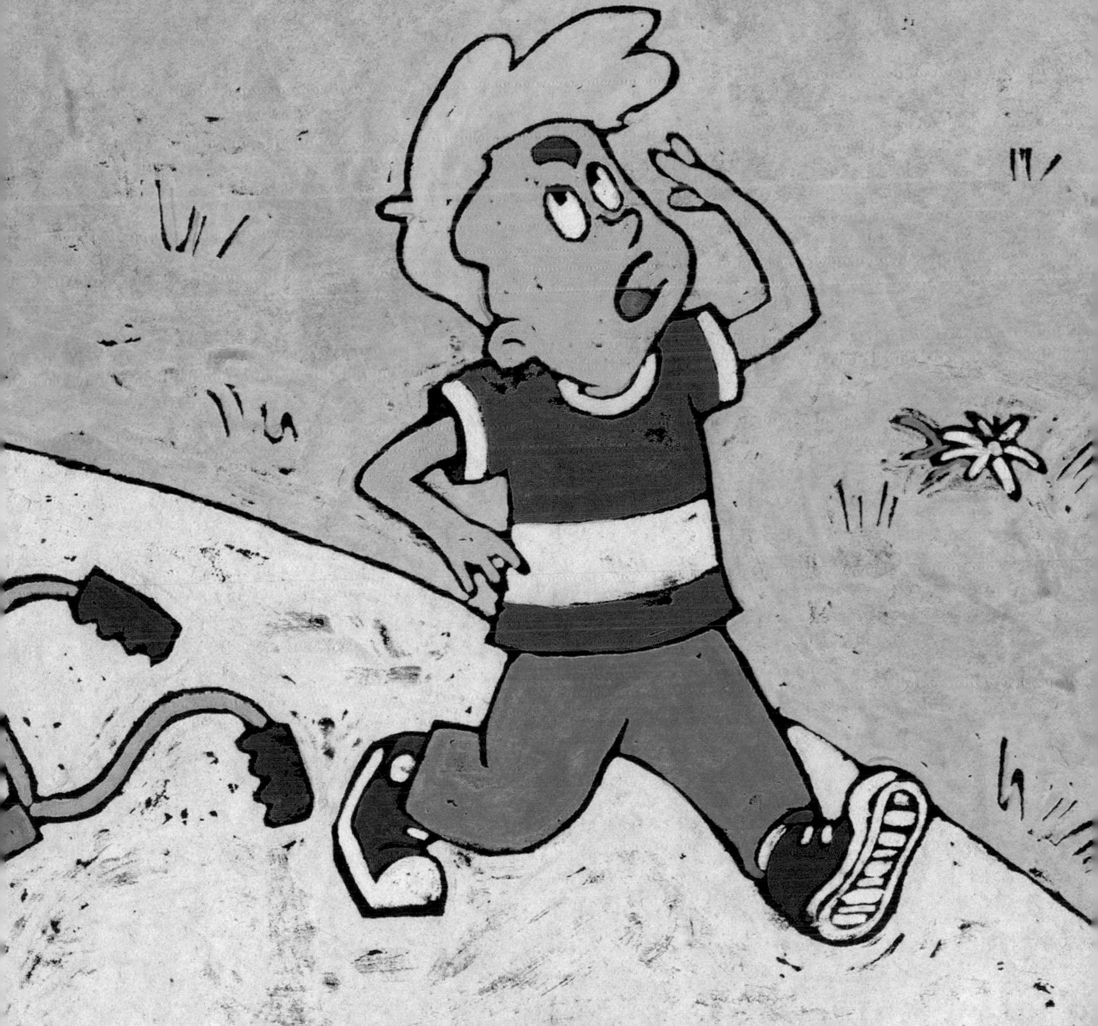

"My head is bleeding!"

"Let me see your head,"
said Jon's mother.

"It's bleeding!"
Jon cried.

"We're going to the
emergency room," she said.

"But you need stitches,"
said the doctor.
"If I put in stitches, then
you'll only have a little scar."

"Can you lie still—
very still?"
asked the doctor.

"I'll give you a shot so it won't hurt," said the doctor.

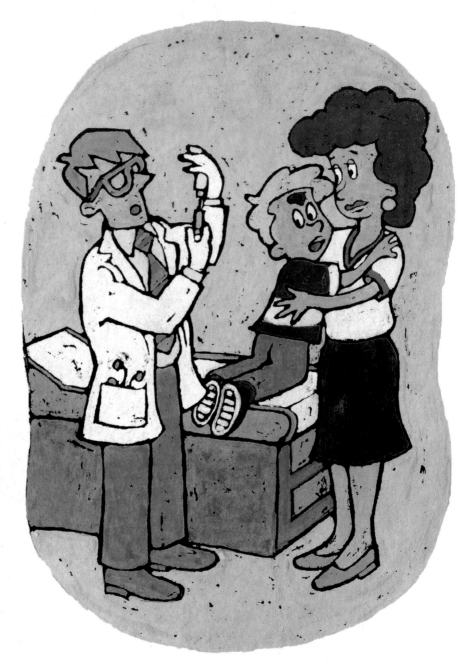

"I don't want a shot!" cried Jon.

"But I can't sew
if I'm hurting you,"
said the doctor.

So Jon got a shot.

The doctor put in six stitches.

"One . . . two . . .
three . . . four . . .
five . . . SIX!"
said the doctor.

"But first you need a bandage,"
said the doctor.

"Then you can go home."

Jon was quiet in the car.
He didn't speak.

He wanted to be in his room.
He wanted to go to bed.

Jon said,
"I don't like blood!

I don't like shots!

And I don't like
stitches!"

"Would you like chicken soup?"
asked his mother.

"Would you like ice cream?"

"No food!" said Jon.

"I don't know what you want!"
said Jon's mother.

"I want my friends,"
said Jon.

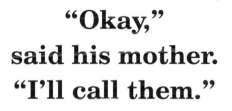

"Okay,"
said his mother.
"I'll call them."

**Jon's friends asked,
"What happened?"**

"I fell," said Jon.

"There was blood everywhere!
I went to the emergency room.

I got a shot.
I got six stitches."

"And do you know what?
I'll always have a little scar!"